Spirit of Technology

by

VOINKS

*Reaching into Cyberspace
can bring surprising
results.*

Copyright © 2017 Voinks

The moral right of the author has been asserted.

Apart from any fair dealing for the purposes of research or private study, or criticism or review, as permitted under the Copyright, Designs and Patents Act 1988, no part of this publication may be reproduced, stored or transmitted, in any form or by any means, electronic or mechanical, including photocopying or recording, without the prior permission in writing of the author, or in the case of reprographic reproduction in accordance with the terms of licenses issued by the Copyright Licensing Agency. Enquiries concerning reproduction outside those terms should be sent to the author.

This is a work of fiction. Names, characters, businesses, places, event and incidents are either the products of the author's imagination or used in a fictitious manner. Any resemblance to actual persons, living or dead, or actual events is purely coincidental.

Bookcover Artist: Paula Harmon

Dedications and acknowledgements:

This book is dedicated to Paula Harmon with grateful thanks for her book cover artistry, nagging and general support.

It also acknowledges the invaluable support and encouragement given by the wonderful community of authors and bloggers.

Books by Voinks

Changes **Olympia publishers**

ABC Destiny **Austin MaCauley publishers**

Short stories by Voinks

Published regularly on my Web site and Facebook author page.

www.Voinks.Wordpress.com

www.facebook.com/Voinks.writer.author

Spirit of Technology

Part 1

My Grandmother was the seventh daughter of the seventh son so perhaps my heritage made me more receptive to the abnormal, and encouraged me to reply to the anonymous message rather than just deleting it.

'Hello. Do you know me?'

'You're in my house so of course I know you.'

Laughing face emo.

'But who are you? What do you mean 'your' house?'

'I lived here when I was young.'

'Your sender address shows unknown. What's your name? When did you live here?'

'I was born in 1898, 20th January to be precise.'

'You're spooking me. You're saying you are over a hundred years old, way before computers were invented. You expect me to believe you know me because I live here now?'

'Sorry. I didn't mean to upset you.'

'OK, so answer my question. Who are you?'

'My name is Andrew, Joseph, Lee, Trevena-Fairfax.'

'Now I know you're teasing, Lee is a modern name. It wasn't around hundred years ago!'

'Google it' came the cryptic reply. 'Gotta go now, catch you later.' *Kiss emo.*

The screen went dead and my first instinct was to feel annoyed that he had cut off before I could prove he was a prankster.

Inevitably I googled 'Lee' and was amazed to find that it was in the top twenty boy's names from a hundred years ago. Then I started laughing at myself.

This guy was just using a magician's sleight of hand to distract from the important topic. He had guessed I wouldn't be able to resist checking his story, and trying to disprove his charade.

Then I had second thoughts.

Was it a scam to keep my computer active while a hacker

gained access to all my passwords and drained my bank accounts?

My immediate instinct was to go online and check my finances but perhaps that was what he was waiting for. He might still be connected and as soon as I logged on would be able to see all the details; the second and tenth letter of my password, Mother's maiden name and the fifth letter of what I had for breakfast.

Was the hundred and fourteen year old person sending me messages real or just a computer scam?

The thought made me realise just how much I had been dragged into this con. Reality check! I was worried. I had always been astute but now I had been taken in like an idiot.

Logging out quickly I worried that the next day would be spent providing a police report, cancelling my credit cards, advising my bank, changing all my passwords and admitting my stupidity at being duped.

When I got home from work I was afraid to sign in, wondering what I would find. Everything seemed normal; junk mail, e-mails from friends and online bills.

Confidence partly restored I even logged into my bank and credit card accounts.

I panicked when I saw an entry I didn't recognise, then realised it was the online company name for something I had recently ordered. I started to relax a bit and wondered if it was just a friend winding me up.

Then he popped up again.

'Hi, sorry I worried you. I only wanted to talk to you and share some memories. Forgive me!'

I knew it was stupid but I couldn't help replying. He seemed so genuine.

'How did you know what I was doing? If you are a hundred and fourteen years old you wouldn't understand computers. You must be alive if you can use modern technology.'

'Everything I know about your time I've learnt from web sites and pictures but I've had years to read and teach myself.'

'I'm still not convinced. You sound so plausible but what you are saying is impossible. How can you even see to read and type with eyes a century old?'

Rolling on the floor laughing emo.

'You've got it a bit wrong! It's true I was born in 1898 but I died in 1933, so I stayed at thirty-five. My eyesight is as good as yours and in my time I was considered quite presentable. By the way, I've always liked blue-eyed blondes and you are a beautiful girl.'

'How do you know what I look like? You've never seen me.'

'You forget, Darling, I can see everything on your computer. I particularly like the photo of you in the navy spotted bikini.' *Smirk emo.*

I blushed but then realised how clever he was at distracting me.

'Tell me,' I said to change the subject, 'how can you see everything on my computer and know about me and the house?'

'It was where I was born and spent all my life,' he replied.

'My family were quite well off and I was spoilt as I was an only child. We had several servants and I had a happy childhood with a private tutor. My parents were both killed in the war. By the way, I'm talking about the First World War, not the second one. Sometimes I forget to explain things like that.'

'How do you know about computers?'

'My father was an engineer, scientist and mathematician. He was one of the first to actually work on the development of what eventually became computers, so I guess I picked up quite a lot of knowledge without even realising it.

'I wasn't even twenty when my parents died and left me the house and an inheritance. I had no worries about money so I spent a lot of my early years on research, and dedicated my life to following in my father's footsteps.'

'What about getting married? Did you have any children?'

'No, I had a few lady friends but nothing serious. I suppose I was considered quite a catch in those days but I never found the right lady so I never married.'

'What happened? How did you end up contacting me through my computer?'

Even as I typed my reply I realised how ridiculous it sounded, but it had become a challenge to trip up this joker.

'Like I said, I continued my father's research and was playing around with using electrical pulses. The next thing I knew there was a blinding flash, a white light and I was floating in the atmosphere.

'For a while I felt nothing and then found myself looking down on my body lying on the floor. It was odd watching my servants running around, fetching the doctor and trying their best to revive me.'

'So what happened then?'

'After that I lost track of things and just drifted in the ether for a while.

'I remember my funeral. It was a revelation seeing the greed of some of my distant relatives when the solicitor was distributing my worldly worth. They were horrified when they realised I had left everything to my old housekeeper. She had been my nanny when I was growing up and was like a mother to me after I lost my own.

'It was almost worth dying to see her face when she realised she was a rich woman. More importantly, she wouldn't be kicked out on the street. I watched as she and her husband took over the house as owners rather than servants. It was probably why I hung around as they loved the place so much and I still felt I belonged there.'

With a start I realised how involved I had become in his story and had totally forgotten that I was actually online with a supposed ghost. Signing off I wondered if I would ever hear from him again.

That night I had strange dreams of Beau Brummel and Regency England, all mixed up with modern technology. I woke the next morning believing I had dreamed the whole weird scenario.

Work was manic so I didn't have a second to think about my peculiar online friend. I was just leaving when my boss returned needing some work done urgently, so it was nearly seven before I managed to escape.

Running late I had no time to log on when I got home, and was only just ready as the cab arrived for my meeting with friends for our usual Friday night get-together.

It was just what I needed after a very stressful week. Laughing and chatting put everything into perspective- especially after a few drinks. I didn't tell them about my new mystery friend; maybe we just had too many other things to talk about.

I was feeling relaxed when I got home shortly after midnight, and with the weekend before me I had no need to get up early.

With the adrenaline flowing after a brilliant night out I didn't feel like going to bed. I switched on my laptop, browsed some social media and was just thinking of closing down when a message from Andrew popped up.

'Hi', he said, 'did you have a good evening with the girls?'

For a moment I was spooked, then I realised that if he could access my computer he could see my diary.

'Great thanks,' I replied. 'What have you been doing?'

'Waiting to talk to you. What was the food like? I looked up the restaurant and it had very good reviews.'

I started to feel uncomfortable. This guy was stalking me and I was replying as if he was a friend so I didn't answer straight away. He seemed to read my mind as he sent another message.

'Sorry, I didn't mean to pry. I'm just interested in learning if the web site matches the reality.'

Immediately I felt ashamed of myself. The poor guy was only living life second-hand, he needed confirmation from real experiences. I was actually beginning to believe what he was telling me. Maybe I had drunk more than I thought.

I was just composing a reply when my computer crashed. I switched off and on, rebooted, tried all the usual options but nothing worked. Frustrated and annoyed I shut down and decided to go to bed, all my euphoria from earlier forgotten. What if Andy thought I was angry and ignoring him because I didn't want to hear from him again? I slept badly that night but after a long, hot bath and a fry-up I felt ready to face the world again. I logged on but was disappointed when there was no contact from him.

I mooned around all day in between checking my e-mails every ten minutes. Still nothing. By early afternoon I felt bereft and realised how much I missed his contact.

I picked up one of his old messages and sent a reply but it bounced back as 'unknown.' It seemed I could only respond to the current message but if he didn't answer that was it.

A pop-up about online dating agencies set me to wondering why he had not found a suitable wife. Maybe he was gay? If that was the case why had he commented on me in a bikini?

Why was I spending so much time thinking about someone I had never met and who probably didn't even exist? Perhaps he had devised this dashing ghost persona as he was too shy to actually talk to women, and I was spending time fretting because he hadn't contacted me online. I must be as sad as he was. I needed to get a life.

All that soul searching didn't stop my heart beating double time when a message appeared just as I was sitting down to eat my evening meal.

'Hi Babe. Your memory is a bit low so your computer can't cope with all the stored junk. Try deleting some old files or download a clean-up programme. It will save you a lot of hassle.'

'Thanks for the computer advice; I'll give it a whirl. Any particular programme you would recommend? And by the way, is everything you've told me a pack of lies?'

'If I hadn't died I would swear on my life I only told you the truth but I can understand you being cynical. If you trust me I can clean up your computer and make it a lot faster. Actually, I could do it without your permission but my parents installed a sense of honour in me, so I'd rather you gave your consent.'

'Andy, you might be the biggest con man on earth but I've already realised the control you have over my system, so do what you like.'

'Do you realise that's the first time you've used my name? Does that mean you believe I actually exist, even if it's only on your system? It will probably take a few minutes but I'll be right back. Don't go away or switch off. Trust me.' *Kiss emo.*

I watched the screen as the processor went through its motions. White lettering on a black background with gobble-de-gook language, all the usual unintelligible computer-speak when loading an update. What had I let myself in for? But whoever this guy was he already had access to my computer so it was out of my hands.

Unable to stand the suspense I went to make myself a coffee, already wondering how much it would cost to replace everything. Just as I returned I caught a final flash of the usual update screens, then it reverted to my normal desktop.

'All done. You should find it's a lot quicker now without crashing.'

Everything looked normal but when I went onto my usual programmes I was amazed when they came up straight away. I had not realised before how many seconds I spent staring at the screen waiting for things to load.

'Everything OK?'

'It looks fine and seems a lot faster. Thanks Andy. Maybe I should employ you as my IT specialist, especially as you haven't mentioned any fee for your services.'

'I just wanted to talk to you without having to wait ages for your reply. To be honest my love, I'm a bit lonely and I look forward to hearing from you.'

'OK, so tell me, where do you live?'

'Haven't you realised yet sweetheart? I live in the house with you.'

'Stop being cryptic. I mean where is your home? Where do you sleep at nights?'

'You could say your computer is my home. It's where I access information, see world news, even what the weather is like but it's not the same as actually feeling the rain on your face, or the wind blowing through your hair.'

'Where do you find e-mail addresses to decide who to talk to?'

'There are plenty of people, especially on the social web sites. It's more a case of deciding who to leave out. At least I have all the time in the world, so I can keep up to date as well as chatting. Being dead has its advantages.'

'Just as I start to take you seriously you throw in a comment like that! So how did you pick me? I don't belong to any networking sites. How do you know I'm not married?'

'I did a search to find out. Don't forget I have access to registrar's records, council registers, tax returns, you name it. If someone exists they are on a database somewhere. You'd be surprised how much you can discover using technology; photos you save, music or films you download, where you book your holidays, even what you have for breakfast from your shopping lists. Need I go on?'

'OK, point taken. I suppose I could do the same and see a photo of what you look like. Oh, I just realised, cameras weren't around when you were alive.'

'Actually they were. I even had a camera myself when I was a child.'

'Can I see a photo of you as you are now or would nothing show up if you are dead? Better still, what about Skype? Then I could see and hear you.'

'That's a thought. I'll get back to you. Ciao for now.' *Kiss emo.*

He was gone and once again I found myself going over our

conversation and how crazy it must sound. He could send me a photo of anyone and I would be none the wiser. If he came on Skype that would prove he actually existed and therefore wasn't dead.

I had started taking this strange relationship with a ghost so seriously I must be really losing my common sense. Determined not to reply to any more messages I closed down my computer and went off to bed.

My dreams that night were of mobile phones turning themselves inside out to take photographs of clouds, which formed themselves into the shape of computers, which grew mouths and started laughing at me.

After such a restless night I overslept but at least it was Sunday.

Despite my resolve I turned on the computer trying to convince myself I was just checking to see if any friends had been in contact.

My heart dropped when there was nothing from Andy, just some junk mail and a few messages from the girls. Feeling a fool I shut down my computer and headed off for the gym. Later, tired but happy I sat down to read. Although it was a good book I couldn't get into it and kept glancing at the silent computer.

Eventually I gave in and switched on, just to feel stupid when once again there was nothing from Andy. Maybe he realised I had sussed his little game but I missed hearing from him. I went back to my book and this time managed to concentrate and follow the plot.

After a while the smells wafting from the oven reminded me I was hungry and I went into the kitchen to check on my dinner.

Gremlin's law. As I came back into the living room I noticed a message -

'Andrew Trevena-Fairfax invites you to be his Skype friend. Press 'Yes' to accept.'

What to do? Sensible head says hit the delete button. My finger hovered over the button and then took on a life of its own by pressing accept. Now I was committed. Well actually I wasn't, I could still abandon but found myself typing,

'OK, now let me see the genuine you! Please don't send me a picture of some twentieth century gigolo. Just be honest with me.'

All evening I kept glancing at the screen, waiting for the jingle that meant I had a Skype message. I checked and double checked that Skype was activated, all to no avail. I went into the kitchen to wash up, convinced that on the 'watched kettle' syndrome there would be a message when I came back. Nothing! About eleven I gave up and went to bed.

******

Part 2

The next day was a nightmare. My boss was in a foul mood, blaming me for other people's errors, the system crashed and I spent hours talking to service providers whose only job was to fob you off by saying you need to contact blah, blah, who referred you back to your service provider.

So I took the flack, tried not to get stressed and wished for five o'clock. Except five o'clock became six, then my manager calmed down a bit and asked 'Is it possible to get this out tonight? I know you should have left an hour ago but I promised it for first thing tomorrow.'

So I succumbed. After all he was a good boss and most of the time we got on well. Again it was gone seven before I left. The day had finished better than it started but I couldn't wait to get home, eat and unwind. Keeping half an eye on my computer waiting for the beep, I jumped up to look when I heard a sound, then realised it was only an advert on the TV.

I was just going to shut down when 'Ping' that peculiar Skype noise.

'Andrew Fairfax is online. See your in-box for messages from your Skype contact.'

'Hi. Sorry to disturb you so late. Just wanted to prove I was real. Enjoy your cocoa.' *Kiss emo.*

'This doesn't prove anything. It's only a message, not even a video. And how did you know I was drinking cocoa?' *Rolling on the floor laughing emo.*

'I told you Darling, I can see everything. Sleep well.' *Kiss and hug emos.*

'Andrew Fairfax is offline.' Aaagh. That man is so frustrating.

Hang on a minute- 'That man?' I'm thinking of him as if he is real, which of course he is, not some cyber ghost. I should have made a video call to him while he was online and seen what happened, but after the day I'd had my brain wasn't functioning properly.

The next morning I logged on to Skype and hit the icon for Andrew Fairfax. He was 'offline'- so much for modern technology providing instant communication.

My journey that evening was a nightmare, and I thought at least Andy didn't have to experience the joys of commuting. Then I realised I was thinking of him as a cyber-person, whereas he was probably suffering the same travelling tribulations as me. At last there came the announcement of a train which would eventually get me home, even if it was by a circuitous route.

'Why didn't you tell me you were going to catch that train? I could have told you it was cancelled and given you the alternatives to get you home long before now.'

'Everyone can be wise after the event. Anyway I thought you knew everything about me. You could have warned me before I got to the station.'

'Sorry, but I can only go on the processed information from your season ticket and the times your ticket registers when you swipe in and out. You don't normally use that station.'

'So what? Paul was leaving so we went for a drink to say goodbye. Sorry I didn't inform you about every detail of my personal life- Not that it's any concern of yours.'

'I didn't mean to interfere with your social life. I was worried when you didn't swipe your ticket at the usual time and thought you might have had an accident. All the hospital databases were clear but I still couldn't help worrying until you logged on and I knew you were home and safe.'

Despite my tiredness and bad temper that actually sunk in.

He had been concerned enough to trawl the hospitals and I felt elated to know he cared, but at the same time annoyed at the intrusion into my life and frustrated he wasn't a real person. I didn't want any more machines. I needed some strong, soft arms and a proper human being to comfort me.

'I'm alright. I'm tired and I've had enough of technology for one day, so I'm going to bed. Goodnight.'

I unplugged the computer without even closing it down properly.

The next morning, in an attempt to salve my conscience, I

logged on only to get the message, 'No connection- Please try later.'

It was another hectic day at the office although thankfully more productive and we even won a major contract. My boss was in a much better mood and acknowledged the contribution I had made. I hoped he would remember the comment when bonus time came round.

I determined to celebrate by having a proper meal and maybe even a few glasses of wine. Firing up the processor I intended to share the good news with some friends but Gremlins law- What's the first thing that pops up?

'Andrew Fairfax is online. You have messages.' Did I really want to talk to him? No! But being perverse of course I had to open them.

'Hi, Darling. Congratulations on the contract. I know how hard you worked for it.'

'How did you know about that? Not even the secretaries have been told yet!'

'Electronic correspondence Honey. You know every e-mail to your superior gets copied to you.'

I was too gob-smacked for a moment to reply. This guy was worse than a stalker, knowing every single thing that happened in my life. Perhaps the best thing to do would be to stop replying, put him in the junk box and cease all communication. Eventually he would get the hint and I could get on with my life undisturbed. So what did I do? Respond!

'Listen. I know you're a technical whiz and I admire your expertise, but don't you think the time has come to stop playing games and just admit exactly who you are? If we actually met for a coffee who knows? I might find I like you and want to be friends.

'All this cloak and dagger stuff about you being over a hundred years old makes you sound deranged and it's making me uncomfortable. I'm challenging you now. Either show up, or shut up. It's up to you. Let me know where and when or the delete box is waiting.'

With that I hit the shut-down switch and then sat gazing at the blank screen, wondering if I had pushed my luck too far and made the wrong decision.

No way was I going to switch the computer on again tonight. I held out until nearly eleven when I convinced myself there might be a message from a friend needing an urgent response.

Andrew Fairfax is offline! Had I blown it completely? It was probably for the best, perhaps I could even find a real lover instead of a phantom one.

The following evening I opened the post, made some long neglected phone calls to my family and then looked at the laptop. I wasn't sure if I was pleased or disappointed when the only communications were the usual rubbish.

Then I heard that annoying but un-ignorable noise. A message. Actually a video call.

My hand hovered over the green pick up button and then there he was.

He looked like something from an eighteenth century romance, but at the same time modern and drop dead gorgeous. For a moment I was too stunned to speak and just gazed at the screen like a teenager on her first date.

'Hi, Beautiful,' he said. 'You look especially lovely tonight.'

'How do you know what I usually look like?' was the only thing my brain could come up with. The smile that lit up his face made him even more attractive.

'I've seen everything from your passport photo to the picture on your security pass,' he laughed, 'and none of them do you justice. What about me? Do I look how you expected? Are you prepared to meet me in the flesh now that you've actually seen me?'

'How can we meet?' I managed to stutter. 'You don't really exist. You're just a cyber being.' Again that devastating smile.

'I've been looking into that. Tomorrow night about nine o'clock make sure you log on and I'll see if what I've been working on is possible. Until tomorrow Darling, sleep well.' *Kiss emo*.

Andrew Fairfax is offline. Was I losing my mind or what?

If he was real why did I need to log on tomorrow night? If he was just a geek what difference would a few hours make? So much for my nice peaceful night; with that expectation how could I possibly sleep? I slept like a log.

When I woke the next morning it seemed like a dream. Reality set in; dress, train, work, train, home, eat, switch on computer, panic and still an hour to go.

What should I wear? Should I put on some make-up or just pretend it was no big deal? Usually time flies in the evening but tonight for some reason it dragged.

I glanced at the clock, eight twenty-seven. For once there were no e-mails. It must be nine by now. Actually eight thirty-one. Had the clock stopped? No, the computer said the same time. This was ridiculous. I would give him until ten whether he connected or not, then I was determined to switch off and have an early night. To pass the time I started playing a few online games. At first I couldn't concentrate but gradually I focussed and even started winning.

Peep. Andrew Fairfax is online.

Without thinking I shut down the game and connected to answer the video call.

'Hi Honey. Sorry to disturb your game, you were on a winner there.'

I felt like a five year old with her hand caught in the cookie jar, although a five year old wouldn't be experiencing the feelings I was, just by seeing his online face again.

I tried to act nonchalant. 'Just passing the time for a bit before I go to bed. How are you?'

'Can I join you?'

'What? In bed?' Oh My God. Where did that come from? I could feel myself turning bright red, especially when his face broke into a beaming smile.

'I didn't actually mean that but who am I to refuse a beautiful lady. Just say the word.'

'Listen. I'll make a deal with you. Knock on my door this very instant and I'll invite you in. Otherwise, stop trying to ridicule me!'

'You're on! All I was waiting for was the invitation but it won't be through the door. I've been testing things out and I think I've found a way but I need your help. If you really want me there just follow my instructions.'

'OK. What do I need to do?'

'Minimise Skype but keep connected to the call and the cam running. Don't worry if your system sounds a bit noisy. I'm boosting the power from inside. Now log onto this web-site: *Wishescometrue/appear-AndrewFairfax/online.now.*

OK, take a deep breath and close your eyes.'

I felt really silly but did as I was told.

There was a loud hum which grew in intensity until I felt my ears would burst then a bang, then silence. I opened my eyes, blinked a few times and then looked back at the screen. Nothing. It was dark and blank.

I twiddled the mouse a few times, hit a few keys at random and even checked the connections. Still nothing. That idiot had exploded my computer!

'Whoops,' came a voice from behind me. 'Seems I overdid the power a bit.'

I spun round so fast I nearly dislocated my neck and just stared open-mouthed. There he stood. All six foot something of him and even more gorgeous in the flesh.

'Hi' he said as he gently turned me round to face him. He put a finger under my chin and carefully closed my mouth which was still hanging open. It felt like an electric charge running down my spine and I shivered.

'Are you cold Honey?' he asked.

'No, I'm fine. It's just that you surprised me. What did you do to my computer? And how did you get in here?'

'Actually, one question answers the other. When I came through the screen I miscalculated the power but don't worry, I'll sort it out for when you want me to go back.'

'What are you talking about? Are you seriously trying to tell me you came from my computer? You must be joking.'

'How else do you think I got here? All your windows and doors are locked up for the night. I promised you I would come and I always keep my promises. So, are you pleased to see me in the flesh?'

Unable to resist I stretched out a hand to touch his shoulder. For a ghost he had very solid muscles. I wondered if ghosts went to the gym and then realised I had to pull myself together before I got hysterical.

'Would you like a drink?' I asked, 'Tea, coffee, or something stronger?'

'Let's celebrate our meeting properly. How about some of that Chablis you bought last week?'

'Sure,' I said as I went into the kitchen to get the glasses and the wine.

When I came back he was sitting on the settee with his long legs stretched out in front of him and looking like every woman's fantasy come true.

I went to sit on one of the chairs but he had other ideas; taking my hand he pulled me down next to him. He was so close I could feel the heat from his thighs even through the denim jeans he was wearing.

Denim jeans? He was supposed to be a ghost born a hundred years ago. They didn't wear jeans in those days. Did they?

He touched our glasses together in a silent toast and smiled at me.

'OK. I can feel the questions so fire away. What do you want to know?'

'How did you know I bought a bottle of wine?'

'Easy. All your purchases are recorded on your payment card, store confirmations and even your collector-point records. Next question?'

'If you are as old as you say you are, how come you are wearing modern clothes? I thought Beau Brummel wore pantaloons, silk shirts and cravats, not jeans, a T-shirt and a leather jacket.'

Laughing he replied 'Can you imagine what your friends would think if I met them wearing that sort of gear? Actually, they probably wouldn't turn a hair but I feel more comfortable like this.'

'What do you mean about meeting my friends?'

'Now I'm here I want to get to know everyone who's close to you, not just through cameras and e-mails.' For a moment his face looked serious.

'Am I presuming too much? Just say if you want me to sort the processor and go back where I came from.'

The computer wasn't working to give him a smiley face emo, so I did the next best thing. I leaned over and kissed his cheek.

'Of course I want to get to know you. How long have you got?'

His face broke into the beaming smile I had already grown to know and love.

'The rest of my life Darling, if that's what you want.'

We spent the rest of the evening getting to know each other, asking and answering questions, discussing our lives, our hopes and dreams and finishing off the bottle of wine.

Suddenly I realised it was three o'clock in the morning. If he was staying, where was he going to sleep? Hand in hand we went up to my bed. I felt totally at ease and comfortable with his arms around me and slept as if there was no tomorrow. In some ways I wished that was true, until I woke the next morning to find him still there cuddling me, so it wasn't a dream after all.

That smile again, that turned my knees to water and made my heart beat twenty to the dozen. 'Morning, sleepy-head,' he said as he kissed me awake.

******

Part 3

Even now, over fifty years later I still get the same tingle. We are as much in love as we were all those years ago when he first emerged from my computer. If you don't know what a computer is look it up. It was the fore-runner of what drives your lives today. I know in this twenty-second century things are different and you might find my story a bit hard to understand, but love existed long before technology.

So don't scoff at ancient history, my beloved grandchildren. After all, if you don't believe in ghosts, how did you get here?

Wink and kiss emos.

AUTHOR'S NOTE

Reviews are an author's lifeblood. If you enjoyed this book please consider leaving a review; even a few words make such a difference.

Thank you.

I love to hear from readers. Please feel free to contact me at

Voinks@hotmail.co.uk

https://voinks.wordpress.com

Other books by Voinks

Changes

US:
www.amazon.com/Changes-Voinks-ebook/dp/B00KFOCKYU/ref=sr_1_1?ie=UTF8&qid=1490285086

www.amazon.com/Changes-Voinks/dp/1848972997

UK:

www.amazon.co.uk/Changes-Voinks-ebook/dp/B00KFOCKYU/ref=sr_1_1?ie=UTF8&qid=1490284747

www.amazon.co.uk/Changes-Voinks/dp/1848972997

Review:
'A thoroughly enjoyable read. Not my usual genre but i was intrigued having read the synopsis. I loved the characters and was absorbed right from the start. The descriptions of the character's experiences were so well written that I felt I was actually there with her. The author clearly has an obvious talent for bringing her writing to life. More from Voinks please, looking forward to her next adventure'

ABC Destiny

US:
www.amazon.com/ABC-Destiny-Voinks-ebook/dp/B0158ZI3EG

www.amazon.com/ABC-Destiny-Voinks-N/dp/1784556963

UK:
www.amazon.co.uk/ABC-Destiny-Voinks-ebook/dp/B0158ZI3EG

www.amazon.co.uk/ABC-Destiny-Voinks/dp/1784556963

Review:
'Another great read by Voinks which kept me enthralled throughout. Voinks has her own unique style and writes in a way that has you guessing at every turn of the page. The characters came to life, connected well. The plot was very clever and I am already looking forward to meeting ABC D again.'

Printed in Great Britain
by Amazon